A Gold Star
for George

By Alice Hemming

Illustrated by Kimberley Scott

For Mum and Dad – A.H

At the Heavenly Hippos Wildlife Park
everyone was talking about the new poster.

George wondered if he would win. He had never won anything before but there was a perfect spot on his fence for a shiny gold star.

It was no surprise when the penguins
won the star for 'Most Popular Animal'.
All the visitors loved the penguins.

They had a party to celebrate.
George was very pleased for them.

The next star was for the 'Tidiest Animal'.
George always kept his area spick and span.

But the lemurs needed a bit of help with their house.

George was always happy to help Seymour – his best friend.

Competition was tough for the 'Best Trick' award. Every animal in the park seemed to have a hidden talent.

Every animal apart from George, that is.

He tried magic tricks, but he couldn't hold the cards.

Gymnastics was impossible.

And he just couldn't master the hula-hoop.

The final star was for the most stylish animal. George felt quietly confident.

But on judging day, all the other animals made a special effort.

"Well done," said George to the winner.

George was pleased for his friends, but that night he gazed at the bare spot on his fence. How would it have felt to be a winner?

George awoke to the sound of muttering and banging. He saw something twinkling on his fence. Something shiny!

Now, surrounded by his friends,
George knew how it felt to be a winner!

The End

A Gold Star for George
is an original concept by
© Alice Hemming

Illustrator: Kimberley Scott
Represented by Advocate Art

Published by MAVERICK ARTS PUBLISHING LTD
Studio 3A, City Business Centre, 6 Brighton Road,
Horsham, West Sussex, RH13 5BB
© Maverick Arts Publishing Limited May 2015 +44 (0)1403 256941

A CIP catalogue record for this book is available at the British Library.

ISBN 978-1-84886-171-8

Maverick
arts publishing

www.maverickbooks.co.uk